MOBY DICK

Herman Melville's

MOBY DICK

Adapted for young readers by FELIX SUTTON
Illustrated by H. B. VESTAL

GROSSET & DUNLAP · Publishers · NEW YORK

NOTE TO PARENTS

Herman Melville's enthralling story of Captain Ahab's furious and ill-fated quest for the great White Whale is one of the great books of all time.

This adaptation of MOBY DICK for younger readers has been especially prepared to retain the spirit and atmosphere of the original book. Here are all the highlights of the original story: Ishmael's arrival in the busy town of New Bedford, his meeting with the weird savage, Queequeg, Captain Ahab with his ivory leg and his mad vengeance, and the fierce sea battle with the great White Whale.

The dramatic illustrations on every page are in keeping with the spirit of this American classic.

When your child is a little older, he will want to read the original story of MOBY DICK, many times longer than this.

ISBN: 0-448-02142-0
1974 Printing

CALL ME ISHMAEL. I was with Captain Ahab on the good ship "Pequod" when we sailed halfway round the world to find the great White Whale, Moby Dick. It was I, standing high in the rigging, braced against the topmost crosstree, who first sighted the white sea beast's spout. I was the bowsman in Captain Ahab's boat when he threw the fatal harpoon that lashed the great whale into such fury that he smashed the ship into driftwood and the small whaleboats into kindling and killed every man jack of the crew and took Captain Ahab with him on his last long plunge into the depths.

I was the only one of the crew who was left alive after that awful experience. And this is the way it happened. I'll start at the beginning.

THE SPOUTER-INN

Whenever I am in the mood for adventure, I go to sea. And so one morning, I stuffed a shirt or two into my old carpetbag and started for Nantucket—the island port off the coast of Massachusetts from which whalers set off to cruise the seven seas.

Arriving in New Bedford, I found that I had to wait for a boat to the island. So I set off down the narrow, cobbled streets of the seaport town, looking for a lodging to spend the night. Soon I came to a queer sort of place, an old house which stood on a bleak corner and seemed to lean into the wind. Overhead, I heard a creaking in the air and, looking up, I saw a swinging sign over the door. The words read, "The Spouter-Inn."

Entering the main room, I found a number of young seamen gathered about a table underneath a swinging whale-oil lamp. I inquired for the landlord and finally found him polishing pewter mugs.

"Well, now, lad," he said when I asked him about a room for the night. "It's all full up we are. But, avast now," he added, scratching his scraggling beard, "I suppose you've no objections to sharing a harpooner's blanket. From the looks of you, you're going whaling, so you'd better get used to that sort of thing."

There seemed to be no other shelter from the clammy night. And so, after a hot meal of beef and dumplings before the roaring fire, the landlord showed me to the room I was to share.

"Now, then," I asked, "where is the harpooner with whom I'm to share this bed?"

"He's a strange one, to be sure," he replied. "Sometimes he doesn't come in until all hours. You just go off to sleep and forget about him."

And with that, the landlord left the room.

I was excited from my journey and sleep would not come. So I lay awake, staring into the dark.

Presently, I must have dozed. For I was awakened by the creaking of the door. It opened. And there, standing in the door-way, lighted by the candle he held, was the strangest-looking man I had ever seen.

QUEEQUEG

He was a tall man, well over six feet, and when he took off his clothes, I saw that he was covered from head to toe with strange, purple-colored tattoo marks. There was no hair on his head, none to speak of, at least. It was shaved as smooth as the palm of his hand—all but a small scalp-knot that twisted up on his forehead.

When he was undressed, he fumbled in the pockets of his coat which he had hung over a chair. From it, he produced a curious little deformed image, which I saw was a wooden idol.

From the pocket, also, he took a handful of wood shavings. Then, setting the small, ugly idol up in the fireplace, he proceeded to light a flame in front of it. Squatting there in the dim firelight, he swayed from side to side before the image and seemed to sing or chant in a low guttural voice.

At last, he put out the small fire. Then, replacing the image in his pocket, he leaped into bed beside me. This was too much for my nerves. I leaped out of bed and screamed for the landlord.

That gentleman soon made his appearance.

"Why didn't you tell me that this harpooner was a canni-bal?" I demanded, shaking from my shock.

The landlord laughed. "Don't be afraid, now. Queequeg here wouldn't harm a hair of your head."

He turned to the savage, still laughing. "Queequeg," he said, "look here. You sabbee me, I sabbee you. This boy sleepee you. You sabbee?"

Queequeg grinned and nodded his big head. "Me sabbee," he said, grinning and slapping me on the back. "Me sabbee plenty. This boy my good friend."

Then we turned in, and I never slept better.

THE "PEQUOD"

After a breakfast of hot coffee and rolls, Queequeg and I set off down the damp streets of New Bedford for the boat to Nantucket.

On the way, Queequeg, speaking in pidgin English, told me his story.

He was a native of Kokovoko, an island in the southwest Pacific. You won't find it on any map—true places never are. Queequeg's father was a chief, but when a New England whaler visited Kokovoko Bay, Queequeg wanted to sail with them as a seaman. At first, the ship's Captain had objected to taking an islander—and such a queer-looking one—as a member of his crew. But when Queequeg showed him how he could throw a spear and hit a coconut at fifty paces, the Captain decided that the chief's son had the makings of a master harpooner.

So for the past ten years, my new-found friend had been sailing the seven seas in whaling vessels.

At last we reached the old port on Nantucket Island—which Indians had used for whaling before the white men came. As we walked along the ancient, weather-beaten wharf, we came to a ship that seemed to be fitting out for a long fishing voyage.

On the deck stood a tall, spare man, dressed in a long coat and wearing a tall hat. One of his legs was an ivory peg, which had been carved from the jawbone of a sperm whale.

"Ahoy, the deck!" I cried. "Are you shipping hands for the voyage?"

"Know anything about whaling?" the Captain—for I assumed that this was he—asked.

"Nothing, sir," I replied. "But I am sure that I'll soon learn. And I've had several cruises in the merchant service."

"Merchant service, my foot!" the one-legged man replied. "Are you a whaling man at heart?"

"I think so, sir. I want to see the world."

"Are you a man," he shouted, "who could pitch a harpoon down a live whale's throat and then jump after it? Answer me!"

Before I could stammer a reply, Queequeg, who was carrying his harpoon over his shoulder, flung it with what seemed to be the speed of light and sank it into the mainmast just above the Captain's head.

"Me whaler!" he cried. "Me harpooner! You sabbee me! You sabbee my friend!"

The Captain didn't move an inch. Queequeg's harpoon still quivered in the wood of the mast. "Come aboard, lads," he said. "My chief mate will sign ye on."

THE CREW

The crew of the good ship "Pequod" was a strange one. There was Captain Ahab, a Nantucket Quaker—he of the ivory peg leg. At the beginning of our journey, he kept to his cabin most of the time. But later we were to see Captain Ahab upon his quarterdeck more often, looking out across the sea with a fixed and fearless glance.

Mr. Starbuck was the chief mate. He was a native of Nantucket and a Quaker by descent. Like the Captain, he too was a tall, thin man.

"I'll have no man in my boat," he said, "who is not afraid of a whale." By this he meant that a useful whale hunter is one who knows how dangerous a whale can be. He didn't want anyone taking foolish chances that might endanger the ship.

The second mate was Mr. Stubb, a man from Cape Cod—happy-go-lucky, easy-going and completely without fear. Later, I was to see him stand in the bow of his boat, when close to the most monstrous whale, and puff on a stubby, black pipe while he hummed a rigadig tune. This pipe was as much a part of his face as his nose, and he was never without it. When Stubb climbed out of his bunk in the morning to dress, instead of first putting his legs into his pants, he put his pipe into his mouth.

Mr. Flask, from Martha's Vineyard, was Captain Ahab's third mate. A short, stout young fellow, full of fight, he seemed to think that every whale was his personal enemy. And it was almost a point of honor with him to kill each one he saw. To him, the great, majestic sea beast was nothing more than a mouse, many times magnified and requiring only a little trouble to kill and boil down for oil.

Each mate commanded a whaleboat. And each had his own right-hand man, his harpooner.

Of the harpooners, you have already met my friend from the far-off South Seas, Queequeg. The other two were Tashtego, a thin, wiry Indian, and Daggoo, a gigantic Negro from Africa.

Both Tashtego and Daggoo could wield their long, sharp-pointed harpoons with as much accuracy as Queequeg. We knew that when our boats came within throwing distance of a whale, the huge beast had little chance of escaping the plunge of sharp steel into its broad, black back.

The rest of the "Pequod's" crew, myself included, were on board to back up this team of skilled hunters. Whenever the lookouts sighted a whale, the whaleboats were lowered and we rowed them to within harpoon range.

THE WHITE WHALE

For weeks after the "Pequod" put to sea, Captain Ahab stayed below in his cabin. The ship drove steadily southward, pushed along by favoring winds.

Then, one morning Ahab appeared on the quarterdeck, where a ship's captain usually stands.

"Mr. Starbuck!" he yelled. "Mr. Starbuck! Assemble all hands on deck! Bring the lookouts down from the mastheads! All hands on deck, I say!"

Starbuck ran to do his Captain's bidding, and soon the entire ship's company was lined up, shuffling their tough, bare feet on the deck and pulling nervously at their tarred forelocks.

Suddenly, Captain Ahab thrust up his right arm. In his fingers was a shiny piece of gold.

"What do you do when you see a whale, men?" he shouted.

"Sing out for him," a dozen sailors cried at once.

"And what say ye?" asked the Captain.

"Thar she blows! Thar she blows!"

"Then look ye!" cried the Captain. "See ye this Spanish piece of gold? It is a sixteen-dollar piece. Mr. Starbuck, hand me that maul."

Taking the maul from Starbuck, Ahab advanced to the main-mast. There, without saying a word, he drove the gold coin, edge-wise, into the wood.

"Now hear, ye!" he cried. "Whichever man jack of ye cries out 'Thar she blows!' and the whale is white-headed with a crooked jaw and three holes punctured in his starboard fluke — whichever man of ye raises me that white whale shall have this gold piece, my boys!"

The sailors leaped and danced. "Huzza! Huzza!" they shouted.

At the mention of a white whale with a crooked jaw, Queequeg, Daggoo and Tashtego, the harpooners, quickly looked at each other as though they were struck by the same recollection.

"Captain Ahab," said Tashtego, "that white whale must be the same that some call Moby Dick."

"Moby Dick?" shouted Ahab. "Do ye know the White Whale, Tash?"

"Do he fantail a little 'fore he go down?" the giant black Daggoo asked excitedly.

"And he have one, two, three — oh, many, many harpoons in him hide, Cap'n, all sticking out every which way?" asked Queequeg.

"Aye, that's him!" shouted the Captain. "He has a hundred harpoons sticking out of his hide like pins in a pincushion. But mine's the harpoon that'll finish him! You can lay to that!"

Mr. Starbuck spoke quietly. "Captain," he said, "I've heard tell it was this same Moby Dick that bit off your leg these five years ago."

"Aye, Starbuck!" shouted Ahab. "Aye, my hearties all round! It was Moby Dick that dismasted me, off the coast of Japan. It was Moby Dick, that accursed White Whale, that snapped off this leg of mine with that crooked jaw of his!"

Then, tossing up both arms, he shook his fists at the sky.

"Aye! Aye!" he cried. "And I'll chase him around Good Hope and the Horn and all the islands of the great South Seas before I give him up! And this is what ye have shipped for, men! To chase that white devil over all the waters of the earth till he spouts black blood and rolls belly up on the waves! What say ye, lads? Are ye with me?"

"Aye! Aye!" shouted the harpooners and the men.

"A sharp eye for the White Whale! And a sharp harpoon for Moby Dick!"

To my surprise, I found myself shouting as loudly as the men beside me.

Then Mr. Starbuck spoke up. "I'm game for the White Whale with the crooked jaw, Captain," he said. "But I came to hunt whales and then go home with casks of oil to make us all rich. I didn't come to hunt my commander's vengeance."

"I'll get ye whales," cried Ahab. "I'll get ye oil enough to make ye rich. But I'll get me the White Whale! That's what we're here for, lads!"

As Mr. Starbuck turned slowly away from the skylarking seamen, I heard him whisper, "God help me! God help us all!"

CHASING A WHALE

It was many long months before we caught our first glimpse of Moby Dick. Meanwhile, our job was to hunt whales and boil the rich oil from their blubber. In those faraway days of my youth, whale oil was the only fuel fit to burn in lamps, the only oil that did not sputter and smoke and create more grime and dirt than light. And when it thickened into a white, sweet-smelling wax, it made the very finest candles.

It would take the oil of many whales to fill all the barrels and casks we carried in our hold.

I was on lookout in the crow's-nest the afternoon we sighted and killed our first whale. From this crow's-nest, high on the top of the mainmast, I could see many miles in every direction.

Now a whale is not a fish in the strictest sense of the word. He is a swimming mammal who breathes air through a spout hole in the top of his enormous head. When he comes to the surface to breathe, as he must several times each hour, he blows skyward a great spout of air, mixed with mist and water. This spout is the means by which a lookout can spot him, even though he is more than a mile away.

On this particular day, I was lazing in the crow's-nest, admiring the fleecy clouds that floated across the bright blue afternoon sky, when suddenly I spied a telltale spout. Then almost immediately, close by the first, I saw two others.

"Thar she blows! Thar she blows!" I shouted — the signal that whalemen have always given.

Captain Ahab stood on the quarter-deck.

"Whar blows he, boy?" he shouted.

I pointed forward and slightly to the right.

"Two points off the starboard bow!" I replied.

"Bring her up into the wind!" Captain Ahab cried. And, obeying his own order, he grabbed the wheel from the helmsman and spun it around. The wind spilled from the great canvas sails and the "Pequod" came around to a dead stop in the rolling sea.

"Clear away the boats!" the Captain ordered. But the crew was already unleashing and lowering the three whaleboats.

I clambered down the ratlines, nearly falling to the deck in my excitement, and took my place at an oar in Mr. Starbuck's boat. Queequeg, his big harpoon at his side, was already standing in the bow.

"Lower away!" said Mr. Starbuck. And the men on deck swiftly lowered our boat into the water.

The two other boats, commanded by Mr. Stubb and Mr. Flask, hit the water at the same time. Casting off the lines that bound us to the mother ship, we bent our backs over the oars. Mr. Starbuck kept up a steady chant to time our rowing.

"Pull, boys! Break your backs! You're not pulling hard enough! Let's beat the other boats to the nearest whale! You can pull faster, boys! Let's see you do it! Pull, boys! Pull, boys! Back, forth! Back, forth! Pull, boys! Pull, lads!"

We rowed until I thought my arms and back could stand no more. The big boat skimmed over the water like a canoe. At last the welcome cry was heard:

"Stand up, Queequeg! Stand up," Mr. Starbuck ordered, "and give it to him!"

Queequeg dropped his oar and snatched up his harpoon. By this time we were within twenty feet of the giant whale who was swimming furiously to escape us.

Queequeg stood poised in the bow of the boat, his harpoon balanced above his head. Then, with all the strength of his great body, he threw.

The harpoon sank deep into the whale's side. At its touch, the huge fish flipped up his gigantic tail and dived. The heavy line, fastened to the harpoon, went whistling out of the tub into which it had been so carefully coiled.

Now the boat was being pulled along at the speed of an express train by the harpooned whale.

"Look alive, lads!" Mr. Starbuck ordered. "He'll surface soon, and we must be ready for him."

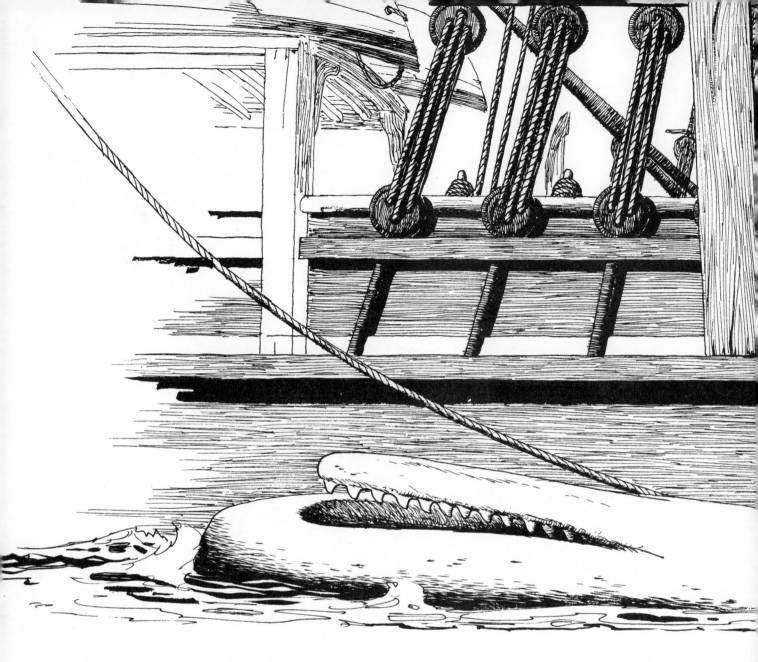

True enough, in a few minutes the great whale came to the surface. Queequeg threw more darts into his broad, black side, and slowly — very slowly — he came to a stop. Blood gushed from the wounds that the harpoon and darts had made. Then a final shower of black blood erupted from his spout hole, and the great sea beast — king of all the ocean wilderness — rolled over on his back and lay still in the water.

"Well done, boys!" said Mr. Starbuck.

As we fastened more lines to our whale to pull him to the ship, I saw that one of the other two boats had already killed its whale, while the second was still being dragged through the water by the beast it had harpooned. Soon, however, it too was hauling a whale to the "Pequod's" side.

WHALE STEAK

At last, the three whales were securely fastened to the ship's side. Night was falling by the time this job was done and the exhausted crews of the whaleboats were lying on the "Pequod's" deck, trying to get back their breath.

Mr. Starbuck came on deck.

"All right, lads," he said. "Lie easy. We'll rest tonight and wait until tomorrow before we try out these beauties."

I had seen that already some sharks were feasting on our prizes as they floated in the water alongside.

"But, sir," I protested, "won't those sharks have eaten most of our whales by morning?"

"If we were in the Pacific, where sharks abound," Mr. Starbuck answered, "we might have no rest tonight. But here there are not so many. So rest easy. You'll have plenty of work to do tomorrow."

"In that case," shouted Mr. Stubb, "I'll have a steak from his small. Over you go, Daggoo, and cut me a big, juicy one."

I had never heard that whale meat was good to eat. I asked Queequeg about it.

"Whale meat good," he answered. "Me have big steak, too. You want?"

There's a first time for everything, I thought. So I nodded. Immediately, Queequeg went over the side, along with Daggoo, and proceeded to cut a steak from the whale's "small." This is the tapering part of the carcass, above the flukes, or tail.

Queequeg broiled the steaks over a roaring fire. I was amazed at how rich and sweet they tasted, very much like the good, red beef we ate back home. But I decided that there can be too much of a good thing. When you look at a meat pie a hundred feet long, it rather takes away your appetite.

THE TRY-WORKS

Catching the whale is only a part of the whaling man's job. The dirtier, messier part, is trying out, or boiling down, the blubber to extract the oil.

The whale's blubber is a thick layer of beefy fat, ten to fifteen inches thick, which covers his whole body. The whale is not cold-blooded like a fish, but warm-blooded like any animal. Thanks to the protection of his layer of blubber, he can swim and live contentedly in the coldest of seas. It is like a blanket that keeps him warm no matter where he goes.

The blubber is peeled from the whale's carcass by long, sharp tools called flensing knives. Then it is cut into thin slices and put into huge metal pots. Over a fire it is "tried out," as whaling men say — until nothing is left but the oil. While it is still warm the oil is stored away in wooden casks.

It took several days to try out our three whales. Then we scrubbed down the decks and removed all traces of blood and oil. When the "Pequod" was spick-and-span and shipshape again, we sailed on to hunt for more whales.

THE "PEQUOD" MEETS THE "SAMUEL ENDERBY"

"Ship ahoy! Have ye seen the White Whale?"

So Captain Ahab hailed a ship that bore down upon us one bright morning some months later. She was flying British colors from her foretop. On her prow was the name, "Samuel Enderby" — and her home port, "London."

Trumpet to mouth, the Captain stood on his quarter-deck, his ivory peg leg securely stuck into the hole that the ship's carpenter had drilled for it.

The English Captain was leaning against the bow rail of his ship. He was dressed in a blue uniform. One sleeve of his jacket was empty. It streamed behind him, flapping in the wind.

"Have ye seen aught of the White Whale?" Ahab repeated.

"Look," the other said. And from within the folds of his jacket, he drew out a slender arm of sperm whale ivory. The hand was a wooden mallet head.

"Man my boat!" cried Ahab. "Stand by to lower away!"

When Ahab and we of his boat crew had climbed to the British ship's deck, the Captain held his ivory arm out in welcome.

"Aye, aye," he cried. "Let us shake bones together. An arm and a leg!"

"The White Whale," Ahab persisted. "He took off that arm, did he?"

"Aye! And that leg?"

"Aye, that he did!"

The English Captain burst out laughing.

Ahab was as stern and darkly foreboding as a summer storm cloud. "Spin me the yarn," he said.

"Well," said the English Captain, "it was the first time I had cruised the Equator. I knew nothing of the White Whale."

"Him called Moby Dick," put in Queequeg.

"Quiet!" Ahab roared. "Go on, Captain, with your tale."

"Well, sir," the Captain continued, "we had spotted a pod of four or five whales and put off in our boats. I was soon fastened to one of them and he was leading me a merry chase. Then all of a sudden, up from the depths, came the body of this tremendous big whale. Milky-white all over he was . . ."

"That was him!" cried Ahab. "Moby Dick!"

"And harpoons, dozens of them, sticking in near his starboard fin."

"Aye, aye — they were mine — my irons!" shouted Ahab. "But go on!"

"Give me a chance," said the Englishman, with a smile. "Well, this old great-grandfather of a whale dashed about among the pod, snapping his great jaws furiously and trying to cut my whale free. Seeing what a noble big whale he was, I wanted to capture him. But before I could get my harpoon raised to throw, he lunged at the boat like an angry bull. There he came, charging at me with the white water making a wave underneath his jaw, and then he ducked his head and brought it up under the boat and threw us all, boat and crew, over his head as a puppy shakes water from his ears."

"But the arm?" cried Ahab. "How did you lose the arm?"

"We all struck out in the water," the Captain went on, "trying to escape his fury. Then he turned and scraped alongside me. And one of the rusted harpoons that stuck out from his side caught me on the arm. Dull and rusted as it was, it trimmed off my flipper like a knife slicing through cake."

"And then what happened?"

"The White Whale sounded and was gone."

"Did ye never cross his wake again?" asked Ahab.

"Twice," was the reply.

"But ye couldn't harpoon him again?"

"Didn't want to try," the Englishman replied. "Isn't one arm enough to lose?"

"Which way was he heading?" demanded Ahab.

"East, I think. But — Gad, man! Are you clean daft? Isn't one leg enough for you, too?"

Ahab turned away. "Avast!" he roared. "Man the boat!"

When we got back to the "Pequod," Captain Ahab strode to the quarter-deck where the first mate had the watch. "Mr. Starbuck!" he ordered. "Make your course east! Due east!"

MOBY DICK

Eastward we sailed — for days, for weeks, for months. When we sighted a pod of whales, we came about and took them. But Ahab was impatient. Nothing was important to him but the pursuit of the great White Whale.

Then, one bright morning, it happened.

Again it was I, Ishmael, who was lookout. I had climbed out of the crow's-nest and was standing braced against the topmost crosstree, on my way to the deck. Suddenly I saw a spout on the horizon.

"Thar she blows!" I cried. Then I saw the broad surface of the sea beast's back.

"White!" I yelled. "White as a snow-hill! It's the White Whale! It's Moby Dick!"

The cry was instantly taken up by the other lookouts and by the men on deck. They rushed to the rail to behold the fabulous whale they had been pursuing so long. Moby Dick was a mile or so ahead. Every roll of the sea revealed his white body rolling and twisting in the troughs of the waves. Regularly, he jetted his silent spout of mist-clouds into the air.

"Luff!" shouted Captain Ahab. "Down topgallant sails! Lower away three boats! I'll go in your boat, Mr. Starbuck! Stay on board and keep the ship! I — Ahab — will kill Moby Dick! Stand by, Mr. Starbuck! Lower away, all boats!"

Soon all three boats were dropped. Ahab was in the lead. I was pulling the bow oar. Queequeg had his harpoon ready.

We were pulling up on Moby Dick when he sounded, sliding under the surface as smoothly as a porpoise, making hardly a ripple. Our boats floated on the still sea, waiting for him to reappear.

Then, peering down into the depths, I saw a spot of white far under water. It grew larger and larger as it neared the surface. I could see two long rows of white, ivory teeth. It was Moby Dick's wide-open mouth yawning beneath the boat.

Then the great White Whale struck. Coming up under the boat, swimming on his back, with his cruel lower jaw extending up out of the water, he crushed the whaleboat between his teeth. The wood of the boat shattered. I was thrown clear. When my head came above the surface, I saw that the boat was nothing more than bits of splintered driftwood. Ahab and all the sailors were thrashing madly about.

Moby Dick was swimming in a circle, round and round the wrecked crew. His great white head, rising some twenty feet or more out of the water, looked for all the world like the prow of a ship with the foaming bow waves dashing against it. Ahab, half drowned by the foam lashed up by the huge whale's thrashing flukes, and too weighted down by his ivory leg to swim, began slowly to sink beneath the waves.

Queequeg struck out in his direction and dived. When he reappeared, he was holding the Captain by the coat collar, keeping his head above water.

We were like this when Mr. Stubb came alongside with his boat and heaved us aboard.

Moby Dick sounded, and was seen no more.

On the "Pequod," when the water had been pumped out of his tortured lungs, Captain Ahab struggled to his feet.

"Which way?" he shouted. "Which way was he going, Mr. Starbuck?"

"East," said Starbuck. "But surely, sir, you are giving up the chase! Surely you aren't going to keep up the hunt for the cruel beast that so nearly killed you today!"

"Ahab stands alone," the Captain shouted. "Alone I stand against this brute of the deep. No more legs will he bite off and no more arms! No more boats will he crush and no more men will he kill! Tomorrow the White Whale dies!

"Mr. Starbuck! Steer your course east!"

THE KILL

When a whale sets off in any given direction, he usually stays true to his course. Sometimes he travels in almost a straight line for nearly a thousand miles.

At daybreak, the mastheads were manned by lookouts.

"Do ye see him?" cried Ahab, after allowing a little time for the light to spread.

"See nothing, sir," was the answer.

"Keep a sharp eye peeled," the Captain cautioned. Then he turned to Starbuck:

"Turn up all hands and make sail! He's traveling faster than I thought! Lay on all the canvas she'll take, Mr. Starbuck!"

The rigging sang. The tall masts bent with the wind. The "Pequod" sliced through the water with a white, foamy bone in her teeth.

All the morning long she ran, the white spume flashing high on either side of her sharp-pointed bow.

"Aloft there!" cried Ahab. "What do ye see?"

Again the answer: "Nothing, sir."

"Nothing! And noon at hand! Does no one want the piece of gold in yonder mast? Faster, Mr. Starbuck! Faster, I say."

Another hour passed. Then came the cry from the crow's-nest: "Thar she breaches! Thar she breaches!"

And breached he had! Rising with his topmost speed from

the farthest depths, the great White Whale burst bodily into view; tossing himself—like a trout caught on a hook—clean out of the water. He twisted upward in the air, his huge flukes piling up a mountain of dazzling foam.

"Aye, breach your last to the sun, Moby Dick!" cried Ahab. "Your hour, and my harpoon, are at hand!"

Then: "Lower the boats! I'll take yours, Mr. Starbuck! Stay aboard! The ship's all yours!"

We scrambled into the whaleboats, each man taking his position. I was in my place at the bow. Captain Ahab stood behind me. The deck crew unleashed the lines and lowered us swiftly into the water. We pulled away from the "Pequod."

At the instant we dipped our oars, a voice cried out from the low cabin window under the stern: "The sharks! The sharks! Come back, Master! Come back!"

And it was so. Hardly had we pushed off from the ship than great swarms of sharks rose from the dark waters beneath us and snapped their sharp-toothed jaws at the oar blades every time they were dipped in the water. We attempted to beat them off as we made our way slowly toward the distant spout of Moby Dick. But the sharks persisted. They beat the water around our boat into a churning foam.

Ahab shook his harpoon high over his head.

"On! On!" he shouted. "There lies Moby Dick! There lies the White Whale awaiting my harpoon! Drive on! Drive on!"

Then came a signal from the "Pequod's" masthead, a downward-pointed arm. This meant that Moby Dick had sounded.

"We'll get him when he surfaces, lads!" cried Ahab. "Only a little while longer will that white devil escape my vengeance!"

But this time, it was Moby Dick who made the attack. Suddenly the waters around our boats swelled slowly in broad circles, then quickly upheaved as if sliding sideways from a submerged iceberg that was swiftly rising to the surface. We heard a low rumbling sound and at that instant a huge white form, all bedraggled with trailing ropes and with scores of rusty harpoons and lances sticking in its sides, shot lengthwise from the sea.

Shrouded in a thin veil of mist that caught the rays of the blazing sun, it seemed to hover for a moment in a rainbow, then it twisted and came straight at us.

"Give way!" cried Ahab to the oarsmen. We bent to our oars and turned the boat aside from Moby Dick's path.

But, maddened by the harpoons that festered in his sides, the White Whale seemed possessed of all the devils in the world. He churned himself into a furious speed and rushed in among the three whaleboats with open jaws and lashing tail.

Before the men in the boats could unlimber their harpoons, the sea beast caught Stubb's boat with a flailing fluke. The force of the blow lifted the boat twenty feet out of the water, smashing it to splinters and spilling out the crew like peas from a pod.

In among the wrecked crew rushed the sharks. In the wink of an eye, the water was a foaming shambles of screaming men **and** snapping jaws. The timbers of the boat swirled round and **round** like chips caught in a whirlpool.

"Where's the whale?" shouted Captain Ahab. "Has he gone down again?"

But Ahab looked too near the boat. For, as if bent upon escaping, Moby Dick was now swimming steadily past the "Pequod."

Then came another cry from the ship. It was Mr. Starbuck, shouting across the wind.

"Come back, Captain!" he cried. "Moby Dick does not seek you! Come back, before it is too late!"

But at that moment, as though catching sight of the black sides of the "Pequod" for the first time, the White Whale charged head-on at the ship itself.

The men on deck watched with horror as the mad leviathan of the deep bore down upon them amid a cloud of mist and spray. On and on he came, faster and faster. Then the great white head struck the ship's starboard bow with such outrageous force that the ship's timbers split wide open and the men were scattered about the deck like tenpins.

Diving beneath the sinking ship, Moby Dick made straight for the boat commanded by Mr. Flask. With a slash of his great jaw, he split it in two.

Meantime, we were bending to our oars, our tired backs straining at every stroke, our mouths open and our eyes wide with horror. As our boat glided over the water the sharks stayed with us. They snapped at the oar blades, leaving splinters in the **sea** at almost every dip.

"Pay them no mind!" screamed Ahab. "Pull on! The White Whale must not escape!"

"But at every bite, sir," I cried, "the blades grow smaller. In a little while there will be nothing left with which to pull."

"They will last long enough," said Ahab. "Soon we will know whether these devil sharks swim to feast on the White Whale or on Ahab! Pull on!"

Again Moby Dick came to a stop and lay still in the water, as though unheeding our advancing boat or the sinking "Pequod." Soon we were fairly inside the smoky mountain mist thrown off from the great White Whale's spout.

Ahab arched his back, raised his harpoon into the air and darted it with a swift stroke into the hated White Whale's side. The steel sank deep into the huge, white mound of flesh, and Moby Dick writhed sideways. The line snapped, and he was free. Spasmodically, he rolled his side against the boat—without crushing it, but with such force that Ahab would have been tossed into the sea had he not clutched at the high gunwale.

As it was, three of the oarsmen who had not seen Ahab throw the harpoon were caught off balance and flung into the water. Two of them clutched the sides of the boat and managed to pull themselves back in. But the third man dropped helplessly astern, though still afloat and swimming. Suddenly there was a great lashing and foaming of the water around him. I saw the flashing dorsal fin of a shark. And then the water was quiet and empty.

As though by a miracle, Moby Dick passed us by. Once again he charged the sinking "Pequod," snapping his jaw and boiling up a fiery shower of foam.

I could hear Mr. Starbuck's cry of alarm. "The whale! The whale! Up helm! Oh, Ahab! Captain Ahab! This is your work! The whale turns to meet us. My God, stand by us now!"

I could see Queequeg in the crow's-nest. On deck, the seamen dropped the tools with which they were desperately trying to repair the sinking ship, and rushed to the rail.

The White Whale came on. And again he rammed the "Pequod" full broadside with his great white head.

The "Pequod" trembled. The mainmast bent, and before my horrified eyes, Queequeg was flung from the crow's-nest like an arrow from a bow and landed in the sea. The "Pequod" split wide open. Sea water poured in torrents through the huge cracks in her black sides.

"The ship! The ship!" cried Ahab.

By this time, the fine big ship, with its thousands of barrels of whale oil stored away in its hold, was foundering low in the water. The starboard gunwales were awash. Men were clinging to the rigging. Waves washed over the deck. The "Pequod" was sinking rapidly. Soon, nothing could be seen but the top of her mast, its pennant still flapping in the breeze. At last, that, too, went under. And our small boat was the only object on the broad, quiet surface of the sea.

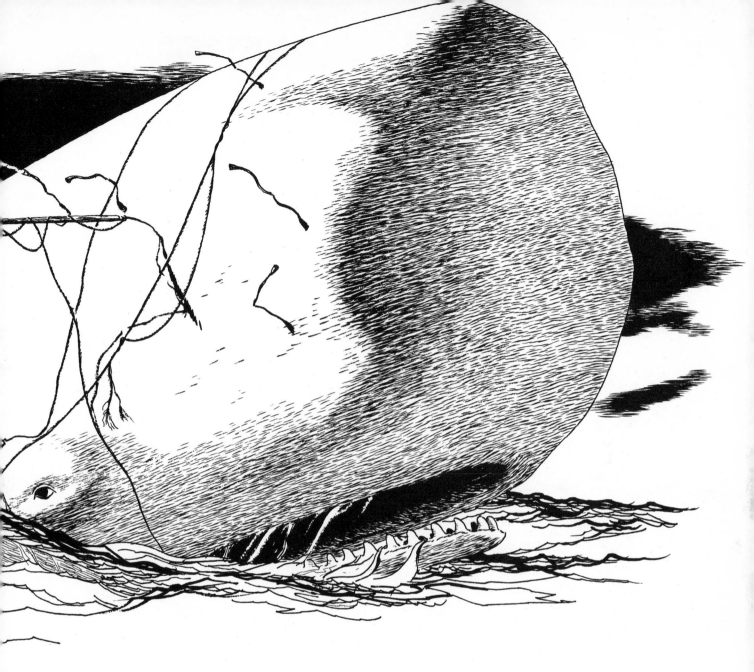

It was then that the great White Whale surfaced, not fifteen feet from our boat and lay for an instant quietly in the water.

With a shrill scream, Captain Ahab hurled his second harpoon. The iron buried itself in the white side of the sea monster, and with a flip of his huge flukes, he flew forward. The line in the boat was fouled. As it reeled out, a loop caught Captain Ahab around the leg and jerked him from the boat.

Moby Dick was dying. No longer had he the strength for swift rushes and mighty charges. From the boat, I could see Ahab going hand-over-hand along the line and, finally, I saw him climb up onto the White Whale's back. He used the rusted harpoons that were stuck into the monster's side as a ladder.

Then he stood up. Pulling his harpoon from Moby Dick's side, he stabbed it in again and again—stabbing, jabbing—jabbing, stabbing—like a madman. But, within minutes, the lines fastened to the irons were tangled around his body in a hopeless confusion.

Then it was that Moby Dick—the great White Whale that Ahab had spent a good part of a lifetime hunting—then it was that Moby Dick finally spouted the fatal black blood and sounded for the last time.

As he went down, one last lashing out of his fluke caught our boat with its full force. The boat was shattered. I was pitched into the water.

When I came to the surface, I had one final glimpse of Moby Dick's magnificent bulk slowly sinking beneath the sea. And there, bound to him forever by the lines of the harpoons that studded his body—and bound to him too, by the even more secure ties of hatred—was the body of Captain Ahab.

RESCUE

I came to my senses later, how much later I do not know. I was clinging to a spar from the "Pequod." A bit of canvas sail was holding my head out of the water.

I looked about me. By some miracle, the sharks had disappeared. There was no sign of life on all the smooth surface of the sea.

I floated like this for two days.

The sun beat down on my head and burned my skin until it cracked and the blood ran down my face. Salt water got into my mouth and I was almost crazed by thirst.

My arms and legs became numb from the chill of the water. I dozed, awoke, dozed again. Night fell and I shivered with cold until my teeth chattered.

I gave myself up for lost. Never again would I see the green hills of my home or the narrow, twisted streets of New Bedford,

or smell the good smells of the food at the Spouter-Inn.

Then, late in the afternoon of the second day—I think it was the second day, for time had no meaning to me—I saw a sail. By great good luck, the lookout saw me in the water. A boat put out. Its crew hauled me over the side, more dead than alive.

The ship was the "Samuel Enderby," its Captain the man with the ivory arm.

"So Captain Ahab met his fate!" he said, when I was dried off and given some hot soup to eat. "He found the White Whale?"

"Aye, that he did!" I said. "And he is with him now."

And so it was that I, Ishmael, am the only man who lived to tell the strange tale of Captain Ahab of Nantucket—and of his mad quest for the great White Whale, Moby Dick.